# A Note to Parents

DK READERS is a compelling program for beginning readers, designed in conjunction with leading literacy experts, including Dr. Linda Gambrell, Professor of Education at Clemson University. Dr. Gambrell has served as President of the National Reading Conference and the College Reading Association, and has recently been elected to serve as President of the International Reading Association.

Beautiful illustrations and superb full-color photographs combine with engaging, easy-to-read stories to offer a fresh approach to each subject in the series. Each DK READER is guaranteed to capture a child's interest while developing his or her reading skills, general knowledge, and love of reading.

The five levels of DK READERS are aimed at different reading abilities, enabling you to choose the books that are exactly right for your child:

**Pre-level 1:** Learning to read
**Level 1:** Beginning to read
**Level 2:** Beginning to read alone
**Level 3:** Reading alone
**Level 4:** Proficient readers

The "normal" age at which a child begins to read can be anywhere from three to eight years old. Adult participation through the lower levels is very helpful for providing encouragement, discussing storylines, and sounding out unfamiliar words.

No matter which level you select, you can be sure that you are helping your child learn to read, then read to learn!

**DK**

LONDON, NEW YORK, MUNICH,
MELBOURNE, AND DELHI

**For Dorling Kindersley**
**Senior Editor** Laura Gilbert
**Managing Art Editor** Ron Stobbart
**Publishing Manager** Catherine Saunders
**Art Director** Lisa Lanzarini
**Associate Publisher** Simon Beecroft
**Category Publisher** Alex Allan
**Production Editor** Sean Daly
**Production Controller** Rita Sinha
**Reading Consultant** Dr. Linda Gambrell

**For Lucasfilm**
**Executive Editor** J. W. Rinzler
**Art Director** Troy Alders
**Keeper of the Holocron** Leland Chee
**Director of Publishing** Carol Roeder

**Designed and edited by Tall Tree Ltd**
**Designer** Sandra Perry
**Editor** Jon Richards

First published in the United States in 2011
by DK Publishing
375 Hudson Street, New York, New York 10014

11 12 13 14 15 10 9 8 7 6 5 4 3 2 1

DK books are available at special discounts when purchased in bulk
for sales promotions, premiums, fund-raising, or educational use.
For details, contact:
DK Publishing Special Markets
375 Hudson Street
New York, New York 10014
SpecialSales@dk.com

A catalog record for this book is available
from the Library of Congress.

ISBN: 978-0-7566-8280-4 (Hardback)
ISBN: 978-0-7566-8281-1 (Paperback)

Reproduced by Media Development and Printing Ltd., UK
Printed and bound in China by L.Rex Printing Company Ltd.

Discover more at:
**www.dk.com**
**www.starwars.com**

# Contents

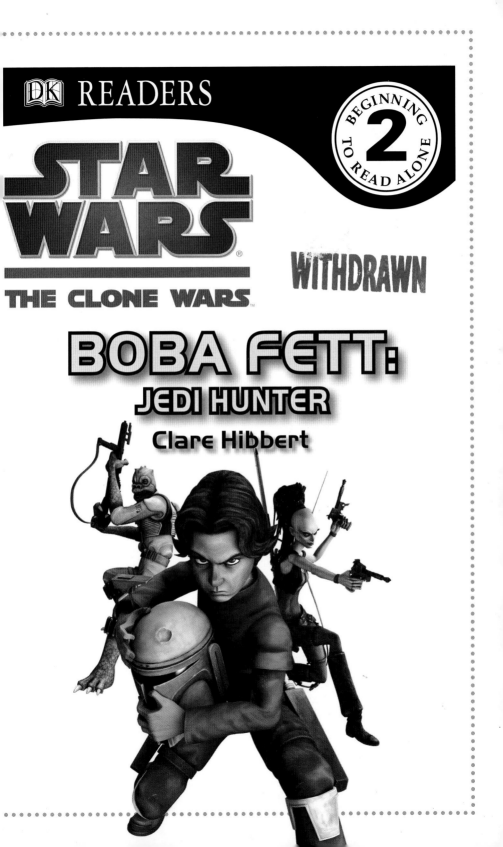

**DK READERS**

2 BEGINNING TO READ ALONE

# STAR WARS
## THE CLONE WARS

WITHDRAWN

# BOBA FETT:
## JEDI HUNTER
### Clare Hibbert

Who is that angry boy?

It is Boba Fett.

Boba wants to hunt down a Jedi Master called Mace Windu.

During a battle, Windu struck
down Boba's father, who was
called Jango Fett.
Now Boba wants revenge.
Can a boy fight a Jedi?
Boba is no ordinary boy.

**Jedi Master**
Mace Windu is a
powerful Jedi Master.
He can use the Force
to give himself
special powers.

Boba is a bounty hunter.
Bounty hunters are paid to
track down people.
Boba works with Aurra Sing.

**Teamwork**
Aurra and Boba team up with other
bounty hunters. Castas is big and
strong. He uses a blaster pistol.

Aurra is a bounty hunter, too.

She is one of the boldest hunters.

She will help Boba find
Mace Windu.

*Aurra Sing*

These are clone troopers.

Clones are exact copies of other
living beings.

The troopers are clones of Jango.

Jango asked to keep one clone
to bring up as his own son.

This son is Boba Fett.

## Clone planet

The clones are trained at a special base
on the planet of Kamino.
Kamino is covered with seas and oceans.

A group called the Separatists
wants to leave the Republic.
Jango helps the Separatists and
their droid soldiers.
The Separatists fight many battles
against the clone troopers.

Mace Windu uses his lightsaber to strike down Jango, Boba's father, during one of these battles.

**Jango's helmet**
After Jango's death, Boba picks up his father's helmet. He swears to take revenge against Mace Windu!

Aurra has an idea.

She knows how Boba can get close
to Windu. He must pretend to be
a clone cadet.

It is risky pretending to be
something you are not,
but Boba is very determined.
No one can stand in his way.

Boba joins Sergeant Crasher's cadet unit. Crasher teaches the cadets how to be troopers. He makes sure that the best cadets have extra training.

## Clone commanders

The best clone troopers become commanders, like Commander Wolffe. He is a brilliant leader. His troops will do anything for him.

Boba needs to wear a special cadet uniform to blend in. When cadets are training on Kamino, they wear cadet armor.

Sometimes, clone cadets wear a gray shirt with a leather belt and boots.

### Insignia
Clone uniforms have special badges called insignia. Commander Wolffe's men wear an insignia of a wolf's head.

Some cadets try to bully Boba.
Jax tells them to leave Boba alone.
He is a good leader. He tries to
make friends with Boba.

*Jax*

Jax doesn't know that Boba is
not what he seems.
He doesn't know that Boba is on
a mission to hunt down a Jedi.

Before Jango died, he taught Boba
everything he knew.
Boba is a very good shot.
He blasts away with the cannon
on the starship *Endurance*.

The Jedi Generals Obi-Wan
Kenobi and Mace Windu are
also on the *Endurance*. Boba is
pleased. His hunt is nearly over!
He may soon have his revenge.

*Cannon*

After Jango died, Boba inherited his spaceship. It is called *Slave I*. Boba has been flying it for years. He is now an ace pilot.

But who is flying it while Boba is hunting Mace Windu on board the *Endurance*?

## Boba's ship

*Slave I* used
to be a ship for
transporting prisoners.
Jango also used it to
transport slaves across
the galaxy. It is full of
the weapons a bounty
hunter needs.

Boba is an expert with gadgets. He has a secret comlink to talk to the other bounty hunters. He uses powerful binoculars to track down Mace Windu.

### Trapping a Jedi
Boba uses his father's helmet as a trap. Jedi Knight Anakin doesn't know there is a bomb inside. However, Windu manages to save Anakin.

Boba has no luck on board the *Endurance*. He must find another way to catch the Jedi.

Aurra commands Boba to destroy
the *Endurance*. The cadets climb
inside an escape pod to get out of
the *Endurance*. Another ship comes
to the rescue. It is *Slave I*.
It is being flown by
bounty hunters!

## No mercy

You have to be tough to be a bounty hunter. Aurra gives Boba a difficult choice: abandon the cadets in space or stay with them in the escape pod and die.

Boba will try anything to get his revenge. He will even take hostages. He captures some of the crew from the *Endurance*.

Mace Windu and Anakin try to
rescue the hostages, but they walk
into a trap. A bomb explodes.
The Jedi barely escape.

Now it is Boba's turn to be hunted.
Jedi Master Plo Koon is looking for
the young bounty hunter.
Boba puts up a good fight,
but Plo Koon is too powerful.

Plo Koon takes Boba to Coruscant.
Boba is face to face with Mace
Windu once again, but this time
Boba is a prisoner.
He failed this time, but this bold
bounty hunter will be back.
Watch your step, Jedi!

# Glossary

**cadet**
A person who is training to be a soldier.

**clone trooper**
A soldier built to serve the Republic.

**comlink**
A mobile device that transmits voice signals.

**escape pod**
A small craft used to escape from a larger craft that is in trouble.

**Force**
A power that flows through the galaxy.

**hostage**
Someone who is kept prisoner as a way to bargain with the enemy.

**Jedi**
A warrior who fights for good.

**lightsaber**
A swordlike weapon with a blade of pure energy.